E Wal
c.1
Walsh, Ellen Stoll.

Mouse magic /

2000.

P9-AQY-384

CASS COUNTY PUBLIC LIBRARY
400 E MECHANIC
HARRISONVILLE, MO 64701

8-8-00

Mouse Magic

Ellen Stoll Walsh

Harcourt, Inc.

San Diego   New York   London

CASS COUNTY LIBRARY
400 E. MECHANIC
HARRISONVILLE, MO 64701

0 0022 0049987 5

A

Copyright © 2000 by Ellen Stoll Walsh

All rights reserved. No part of this publication may be reproduced or transmitted in any form or by any means, electronic or mechanical, including photocopy, recording, or any information storage and retrieval system, without permission in writing from the publisher.

Requests for permission to make copies of any part of the work should be mailed to: Permissions Department, Harcourt, Inc., 6277 Sea Harbor Drive, Orlando, Florida 32887-6777.

Library of Congress Cataloging-in-Publication Data
Walsh, Ellen Stoll.
Mouse magic/Ellen Stoll Walsh.
p.   cm.
Summary: Kit and the Wizard experiment with colors, finding that some colors vibrate when placed next to each other.
ISBN 0-15-200326-6
[1. Color—Fiction. 2. Magic—Fiction. 3. Wizards—Fiction.] I. Title.
PZ7.W1675Mne   2000
[E]—dc21   98-51129

First edition
F E D C B A

Printed in Singapore

The illustrations in this book are cut-paper collage.
The display and text type were set in Palatino.
Color separations by United Graphic Pte. Ltd., Singapore
Printed and bound by Tien Wah Press, Singapore
This book was printed on totally chlorine-free Nymolla Matte Art paper.
Production supervision by Stanley Redfern and Pascha Gerlinger
Designed by Ivan Holmes

For Sique and Andy Spence,
George Stoll, Grace Zaccardi,
and Megan Jenkins
all color magicians

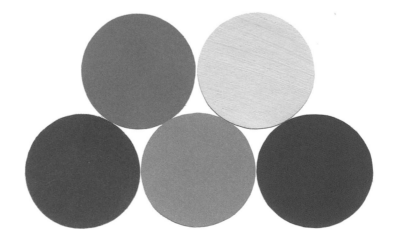

"Hi, Wizard," said Kit. "Come see my favorite colors."

"Well, what do you know," said the wizard, "your favorite colors are magic!"

"I don't think so," said Kit. "These are nice, ordinary, everyday colors."

"Yes," said the wizard, "nice, ordinary, everyday, *magic* colors."

"You shouldn't tease," said Kit.

The wizard laughed. "Look, I'll show you. Here are your colors—red, yellow, and blue. Out of the three, pick any two."

Kit sighed. "I suppose blue and yellow are as good as any."

"Good," said the wizard. "Red's left over. Now I'll mix blue and yellow…"

"To make green," said Kit.

The wizard looked surprised.

Kit smiled. "I learned it from a book, and that's not magic."

"Watch this," said the wizard. "Look what green can do with red."

"They're quivering! How do you do that? Can I try?"

"Sorry, Kit, but magic is wizards' work. Watch, I'll show you another."

"At least tell me how the colors move," said Kit.
"With *magic,*" said the wizard. "Stare at them and see what happens."

Kit laughed. "Well, they move, that's for sure. But how?"

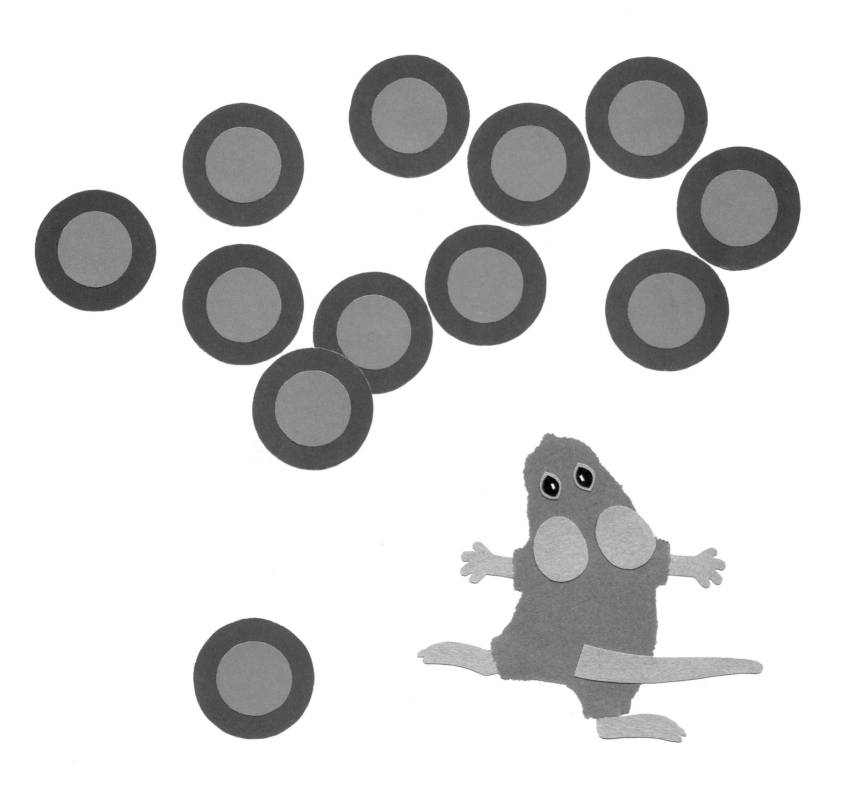

"Will it work with two different colors?" Kit asked. "You said pick any two."

"Let's find out," said the wizard. "What colors do you choose?"

"What about red and yellow to make orange—with blue left over?"

So the wizard mixed orange from red and yellow . . .

. . .and put it with blue.

"What colors!" said Kit. "They can't stay still, either.
Please let me try."

"You are not a wizard, Kit. But watch. I'll show you another."

"Colors can't really move. It's just a trick."

"Are you sure?" asked the wizard.

"Pretty sure," said Kit.

"There are two colors we haven't tried yet," said Kit. "How about red and blue with yellow left over?"

"OK," said the wizard. "Let's finish what we've started."

"Red and blue make purple," said Kit. "Show me what purple and yellow can do."

So the wizard mixed blue and red to make purple . . .

. . .and he put it with yellow.

"Oh," said Kit. "They're doing it, too. Please do one more."

The wizard sighed. "Look, here's the last one. I'm getting sleepy."

"Not me," said Kit. "I really want to try it myself."

"This is not mouse magic, Kit," said the wizard. "And you are still not a wizard."

"But I've been watching a wizard," said Kit.

The wizard shrugged.

"Then try," he said. "I'll take a nap."

Kit tried.

The wizard opened an eye. "Well?" he said.

Kit laughed. "I can do it! It's magic, but the magic is in the color, not in the wizard!"

Author's Note

Red, yellow, and blue are *primary colors.* If you combine two primary colors, you'll get a *secondary color* (for example, mixing blue and red makes purple, a secondary color). If you combine a secondary color with a primary color, you'll get a *tertiary color* (for example, mixing blue and green makes blue-green, a tertiary color). The color wheel is a circular diagram that can be expanded to show all the colors in the spectrum. The diagram below shows a simple color wheel. Colors opposite one another on the color wheel are called *complementary colors.* If you place any two complementary colors together, they will jump around for you, just as they did for Kit. Theoretically. Not all colors are pure enough to work. You need to experiment. Just like Kit.

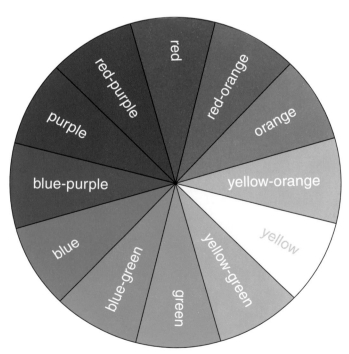

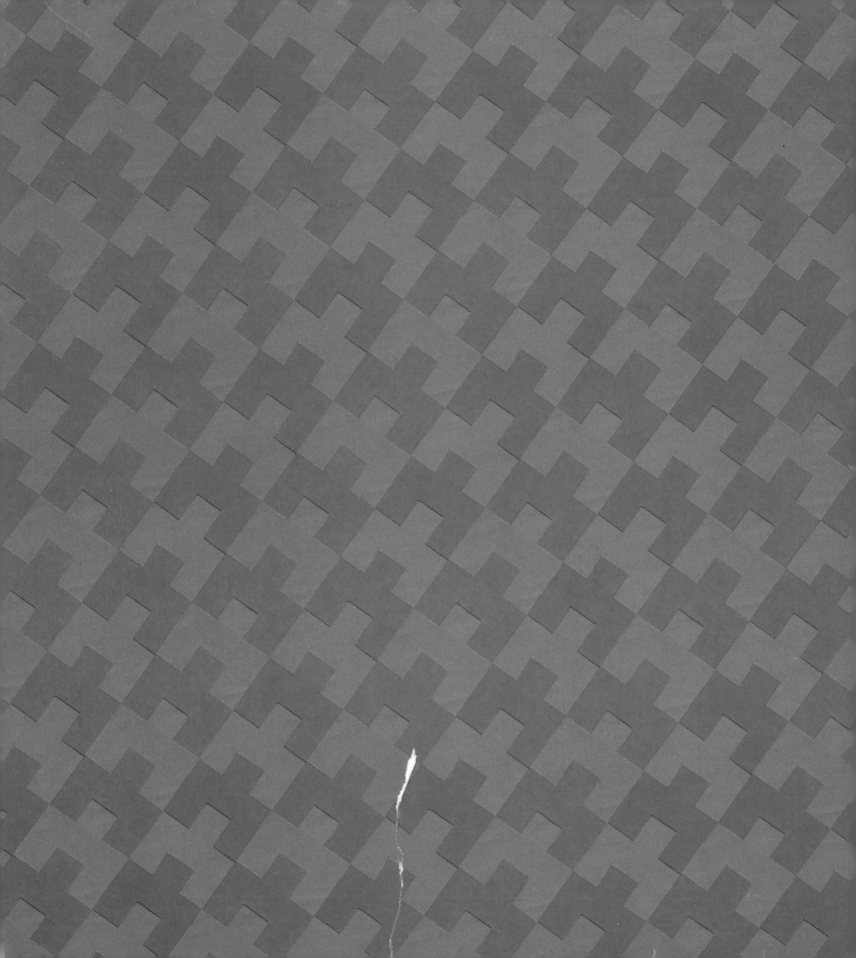